# Grim, Grunt and Grizzle-Tail

## A Story from Chile

Retold by Fran Parnell · Illustrated by Sophie Fatus

## Barefoot Books

### Step inside a story

# Contents

# CHAPTER 1

# The Orange Princesses

Long ago and far away, there lived a king. His people loved him, his palace was filled with gold and his corn grew ripe in the hot summer sun.

But, oh my goodness! What was he to do with his three naughty daughters? All day long, they played cheeky tricks.

Follow me!

They tied the llamas' tails together.
They hid crickets in the king's bed. And
they never stopped teasing Pedro, the boy
who did all the hard work around the
palace. They hid his broom, they swopped
his shoes and left muddy hand-prints on
the palace wall.

One day, the king lost his temper.
'You're just too bad!' he cried. 'I shall
turn you into oranges for a year and a day.'

And — pling! — it was done. The girls had gone. Instead, three beautiful golden oranges hung from the orange tree in the palace garden. The king put a guard under the tree to make sure that his daughters were safe.

I'm so important.

For a long time, the palace was very peaceful and all was well.

But the story of the three orange princesses passed in whispers from mouth to ear. It got louder and louder, until at last, deep underground in the Land of Monsters, the creatures who lived there heard it too.

In that land lived three brothers called Grim, Grunt and Grizzle-Tail. The brothers were as horrible as their names. Each one had the head of an enormous bull.

Sharp white tusks poked from their mouths. Their long tails were angry snakes that lashed and thrashed. Scaly wings flapped on their backs. And they could run faster than the wind on their puma feet.

The eldest brother, Grim, shouted,
'I want an orange princess! Go and get
one for me, shorty.' He gave his littlest
brother a push and a shove. With a sigh,
Grizzle-Tail sprang on his puma feet into
the world above.

Get a move on, shorty!

# CHAPTER 2

# A Fright iN the Night

Under the orange tree, the guard was yawning. 'It's so boring, guarding these oranges night and day,' he muttered. 'I wish something exciting would happen.'

Be careful what you wish for. There was a flapping of scaly wings, a horrible roar and out of the night flew Grizzle-Tail. The guard ran screaming for the hills. Grizzle-Tail reached out a clawed paw and snatched the nearest orange. Then off he flew, back home to the Land of Monsters.

The king was very upset. He offered a reward to anyone who could find his stolen daughter and he sent another man to guard the tree.

Back in the Land of Monsters, Grim
was happy with his princess, but Grunt
was jealous. 'I want an orange princess
too!' he bellowed. 'Go and get one for me,
baby-face.' And he gave his littlest brother
a push.

I love my orange...

With a roll of his eyes, Grizzle-Tail leapt up into the world above on his puma feet.

Under the orange tree, the second guard was huffing and puffing. 'I'm so bored!' he groaned. 'I wish something exciting would happen.'

I'm bored.

Wishes can be dangerous. There was
a flapping of scaly wings, a horrible roar
and out of the night flew Grizzle-Tail.

Yelling in terror, the guard raced away
down the road. Grizzle-Tail reached out a
clawed paw, snatched a second orange,
soared high into the sky and flew home
with his prize.

The next morning, fat, wet tears rolled down the king's cheeks. He offered a bigger reward, but nobody knew where his stolen daughters were. No one wanted to guard the tree any more, either — it was far too frightening.

Now, Pedro missed the princesses too. They had teased him, but the palace was too quiet without their noise and chatter and cheeky tricks. He stood up strong and tall and went to the king.

'I will look after the orange tree,'
Pedro said in his bravest voice.

'You can try if you like,' said the king.
'Here is a sword. Guard the tree carefully,
because if my last daughter is also stolen,
I shall chop off your head.'

I'll do my best.

# CHAPTER 3

# The Monster's Trail

Grim and Grunt were happy with their beautiful fruit. 'You must have an orange princess too!' they shouted at Grizzle-Tail. 'Go and get one!' And they shoved their little brother backwards and forwards, until at last he shouted, 'Oh, all RIGHT! I will fetch the last princess.' And off he flew.

Under the orange tree, Pedro watched the sun set. He listened hard, held his sword tight and waited. Suddenly, with a horrible roar, Grizzle-Tail flew out of the darkness, his long claws stretching for the last golden orange.

Pedro's heart thumped in his chest, but he jumped up and hit the monster with his sword. 'OWWW!' howled Grizzle-Tail. The sword had cut his shoulder. But still he grabbed the last orange and flew away with it into the sky.

Poor Pedro! He had done his best,
but the last orange was gone. He did
not want his head chopped off, so he ran
away. Then he noticed something odd.
Here and there, spits and spots, drips and
drops of the monster's blood had fallen in
the road.

Pedro cheered up. 'At least I can follow the monster's trail,' he thought. 'I'll see if I can catch him.'

Pedro walked and walked. Soon he bumped into the two guards.

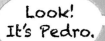

Look!
It's Pedro.

'I'm following the monster's trail,' said Pedro. 'Why don't we look for him together? If we can find the princesses, the king will reward us all instead of chopping off our heads.'

A greedy look crept over the guards' faces. They said they would help Pedro, but in secret they made a plan to kill him and have all the reward for themselves.

The trail ended at a great big rock. Under the rock was the deepest, darkest well in the world. The guards' teeth chattered. 'We're not going down there!' they whispered.

Pedro looked into the darkness and his head spun like a cartwheel. But he said, 'Lower me down, lads. We have to find those princesses.'

# CHAPTER 4

# INto The WeLL

There was a bucket at the top of the well, with a great loop of rope tied onto the handle. Pedro climbed in, and the guards lowered him down into the hole.

'Tug the rope three times when you want us to pull you up,' the guards said to Pedro. They gave each other a sneaky look and grinned.

Down, down, down went Pedro.
The darkness was so thick it was hard
to breathe. Just as he was about to give
up, Pedro saw a tiny light at the bottom.

What a relief! At last, the bucket
bumped down onto the ground. Pedro
had reached the Land of Monsters.

How deep is this well?

All around were craggy mountains.
Far above was a smudge of blue sky and
standing on the other side of a green
cornfield was a huge castle.

Pedro banged on the castle door.
He took a deep breath and lifted his
sword, ready to fight.

The handle rattled and the door creaked open. There stood the three princesses. A year and a day had passed since the king had first changed them into oranges. The spell had broken.

'Pedro!' said the princesses. 'We want to go home. Help us get away from these horrible monsters.'

The girls had been playing their old
tricks on Grim, Grunt and Grizzle-Tail and
the monster brothers were tired out.

Grim and Grunt were fast asleep. It
only took a moment for Pedro to tiptoe in
and chop, chop, chop off their heads!

But Grizzle-Tail could not sleep. His shoulder still hurt where Pedro's sword had hit him. Pedro stood in front of him, waving his sword and looking fierce. But Grizzle-Tail was not angry. He was very happy to see Pedro.

'Dear Pedro!' he said, and he threw
his paws around the boy. 'You've got rid
of my bullying brothers. I never wanted to
steal those tricky princesses.

'Take the girls home and I will be
grateful to you forever. And if you
ever need my help in return, just shout
"Grizzle-Tail!" three times.'

Pedro thought that underneath the claws and tusks and scaly wings, the littlest monster was not so bad.

He took the princesses to the well. They climbed into the bucket, tugged the rope three times and the guards pulled them out of the well.

At last the bucket was ready for
Pedro, but, just as he was about to climb
into it, he heard the guards whisper
something. It did not sound kind.

Pedro remembered how greedy they
had looked when they were following
the monster's trail. He remembered their
sneaky looks as he went down into the
well. All of a sudden, he felt very worried.

# CHAPTER 5

# A Horrible Surprise

Pedro did not climb into the bucket.
Instead, he put a big stone into it and
tugged the rope three times. Then he waited.
Up, up, up went the bucket; but when
it was higher than the treetops, down
it tumbled, and CRASH! went the stone,
smashing into a thousand pieces.

Pedro knew that the guards had betrayed him. Now they would take the princesses back to the palace and claim the reward for themselves. He would be stuck at the bottom of this hole forever and never get home again. Pedro was so upset that he lay down and sobbed.

I'll never get home!

Wait! What had he forgotten? Pedro
wiped his eyes and blew his nose. The
monster had promised to help. Could
Pedro trust him? He decided to find out.

'Grizzle-Tail! Grizzle-Tail! GRIZZLE-TAIL!'
shouted Pedro.

Before the words were out of Pedro's mouth, Grizzle-Tail was by his side. When he heard the story of the wicked guards, he gave a roar that shook the rocks.

'Climb on my back,' he growled. 'We will catch them before they get home.'

Pedro scrambled onto the monster's back, and with one huge leap, Grizzle-Tail sprang into the world above. He flew towards the palace, faster than the wind. The dust billowed, the air howled and Pedro clung to the monster for dear life.

They were at the palace gates just in time! The princesses had stepped inside, and the guards were about to follow. With a flapping of scaly wings and a horrible roaring sound, Grizzle-Tail pounced.

CRUNCH! CRUUUNCH! Grizzle-Tail gobbled up the guards.

Pedro slid off the monster's back
and together they walked into the palace.
Pedro explained how Grizzle-Tail had
helped him and become his friend.

And of course, the king was overjoyed
to see his daughters. He hugged them and
kissed them.

He rewarded Pedro with gold galore.
And he promised never to turn anyone
into an orange again.

I love you.